NICHOLAS
AND HIS INCREDIBLE EYESIGHT

A BOY NAMED NICHOLAS AND HIS ADVENTURE IN THE BIG POLLUTED CITY.

SOTIRIOS PAPATHANASIOU

SEE THE AIR

This book was printed on paper from sustainably managed forests.

Interior Design & Cover Design by: Sotirios Papathanasiou
Illustrations by: Shallu Narula
Editing by: Sotirios Papathanasiou
Consultants: Keriann Saraceno, Michael Saraceno, Kerwin Chang
Printing House: printcolor.es

ISBN: 978-84-697-5270-8
AL 1677-2017

First Edition September 2017
Printed in Spain

Be someone special

Nicholas was an 8 years old boy who was born in Oban, Scotland. A small beautiful town in the west coast of Scotland. Oban means "The Little Bay" in Scottish Gaelic. It has a small population of 9,000 people, but during summer the town can host to up to 20,000 people. The quality of life in the town is high due to the lack of pollution. Fresh air, organic food and clean water are essential for a great life.

Nicholas was a boy of average height and medium build, but he had beautiful green eyes and brown hair. He was living a normal healthy life in the town. He was an active and kind boy as he enjoyed practicing sports at the local sport centre with his friends. Although his favourite activity was golf, he was also keen on football. However, he had had some special abilities that he was unaware of at the moment.

One day his parents told him that soon they will have to move to London because his mother found a better and more profitable job.
A city with a lot of opportunities.

Nicholas was so exited to live in a big city such as London. He had heard about many fantastic things about the City from his teachers and television. However, he was also sad to leave his friends and the unique place where he used to live.

Fortunately, kids don't stay sad for a long time, so a few minutes later he was happy again and ready for his new adventures in the city of London.

The moving day had come. Nicholas sat in the back seat of the car, he put his seatbelt on and he didn't blink once from Oban to London because he was constantly looking out of the window. He wanted to see and learn as much as possible.

The trip was 10 hours long, his father and mother were driving in shifts and when they arrived in London it was already late at night, so they went directly to their new home. Nicholas had fallen asleep. Quietly, his father carried him in his arms to his bedroom and put him to sleep on his new bed.

The next day Nicholas woke up full of energy, but he had a strange sensation in his eyes. He didn't pay a lot of attention at that moment, so he just washed his face with some fresh water in the bathroom sink. Then, he went to the kitchen for breakfast, where his parents waited him.

The following two days the family stayed inside the house as they were tidying up the rooms and getting ready for the beginning of their new life in London.
A new season and school for Nicholas and a new workplace for his mother. His father was a writer and he used to work from home.

The first day at school had come. Nicholas was accompanied by his father and they went there on foot.
Nicholas's eyes started to feel weird again, but he didn't say a word to his father. The sensation wasn't painful at all, but definitely wasn't normal either.

Although at school he made many new friends because he was a sociable boy, his eyes continued tickling him more and more as the days were passing by. Nicholas's school was in a busy area of London with a lot of traffic around, but Nicholas still didn't say anything to anyone. At home the symptoms were weaker and less annoying, so he was able to relax and not think about them a lot.

The days passed with the same strange sensation in his eyes when suddenly one day at school he was able to see the air around him more clearly than ever before. Small particles were floating everywhere in different shapes, sizes and colours. His first reaction was to hold his breath for a few seconds, as he could see these particles entering inside him through his nose and mouth.

Then he asked his friend discreetly if he could see the same things floating in the air. Unfortunately, his friend wasn't able to and he didn't understand his question, so he decided to go to the bathroom and wash his face. While Nicholas was going to the bathroom, he was trying to avoid the particles in the air.

He opened the bathroom door and as he was coming closer to the sink, he was noticing on the mirror that his eyes weren't green any more, but bright blue. He stood there for a minute looking at himself on the mirror until he heard a noise from a bathroom tank. Rapidly, he went to the teachers' office and asked his teacher to call his dad because he wasn't feeling well.

When his dad arrived, he immediately noticed the colour shift in Nicholas's eyes. Nicholas didn't mention to his father that he could see the particles in the air. He just told him that his eyes were tickling him when suddenly, they changed colour.

His father called his mother and they decided to visit an ophthalmologist, who is a specialist eye doctor. Although Nicholas was calm about the fact that his eyes were different now, he was anxious because he could see the unknown particles in the air. Wondering what they were.

The ophthalmologist told them that everything seemed perfectly fine and his eyes were healthy. She even asked them if they were sure his eyes changed colour because she couldn't spot any anomalies or flaws. After that, his parents felt calmer. Nicholas was already calm, but he was still wondering. Once more, he didn't mention anything about the particles because he believed they were going to disappear soon.

At home Nicholas was tired after a long day at school and at the doctor's office. Later on, he took his tablet to play a game called the "PM Invasion". The game was about some tiny alien creatures that tried to invade different cities and poison their ecosystems.

Suddenly, he had an epiphany to search on the vast Internet for something relative to his vision. He tried to write some terms on a search engine like Google, but he didn't succeed on finding something similar of what he was seeing. He didn't lose his passion, so he took a piece of paper and a pencil and drew an image of what he saw that morning, at school, with a great detail.

The following day, Nicholas woke up, got ready really fast and he couldn't wait for his dad to drop him off at school. At school, he greeted his friends quickly and he went straight to the teachers' office where he found his science teacher. Although Mr Brown got a bit surprised to see him so early inside the office, he also saw Nicholas's face full of desire to learn something.

Nicholas took the drawing out of his pocket and asked Mr Brown if he knew what those things were. His teacher asked him where those things were from and Nicholas answered loud and clear, "In the air!" A few seconds of silence followed while his teacher was researching on-line and then Mr Brown shouted, "Those are air pollutants, Nicholas! Now Look at my computer screen". Nicholas looked the images of some of the most common air pollutants on the screen and directly asked his teacher again, "So why do I see these pollutants every day, especially when I am at school?"

- Mr Brown said, "What do you mean you see these pollutants?"
- Nicholas replied, "I see them everywhere and especially here at school, I see them with my own eyes."
- Mr Brown continued, "But you need a good microscope to see them and special instruments to detect them!"
- Nicholas said, "I don't know Mr Brown, please help me!!!"

As they continued to talk Nicholas explained to Mr Brown what happened the previous day and the colour change that his eyes had experienced.

The science teacher decided to help him, so he brought a special instrument to measure the air pollution at school. He wanted to see if Nicholas was telling the truth and if he really had the ability to see the air pollution.

They started some experiments by walking around the school while holding the instrument and taking measurements various times during the day. To his teacher's surprise Nicholas could indeed see the air pollution. The instrument showed a great correlation with what Nicholas's eyes could see.

Nicholas was able to draw the pollutants in fine detail. He drew mostly Particulate Matter which were emitted by cars on the streets and the chimneys. Particulate Matter, also known as PM, are small particles which are very harmful for the respiratory system. The drawings were the proof that Nicholas had an amazing gift.

These are the pollutants that Nicholas could see with his incredible eyesight. You can compare the size of a human hair and the sizes of the pollutants under the microscope.

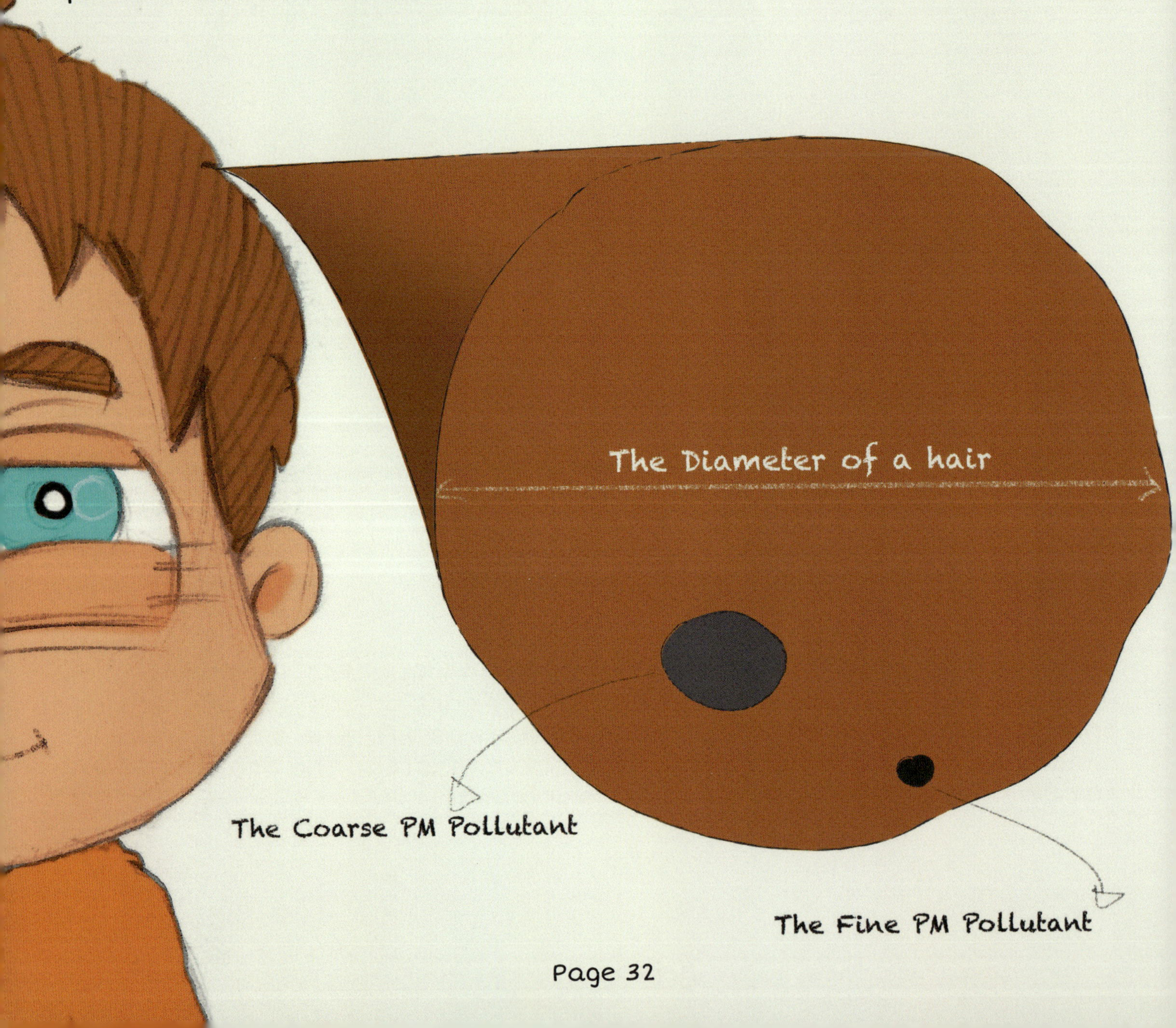

Nicholas and Mr Brown knew that they had to do two things. First, they had to tell Nicholas's parents about his incredible eyesight and secondly, they had to inform the school board about the high air pollution and the danger they were facing every day at school.

In the beginning, Nicholas's parents couldn't believe that their boy had a special power, but they accepted the fact and they supported him as much as they could. The mother and the father hugged their son and told him that they love him unconditionally and they were really proud of him.

At school, when kids learnt that Nicholas had an incredible eyesight, they all raised him together high with their hands and greeted him one by one. Although many of the kids didn't know what PM (Particulate Matter) is, they definitely knew that pollution was very harmful and had to keep it away from school.

The school board listened carefully to the science teacher, Mr Brown and our hero, Nicholas. Then the school board spoke immediately with the City Hall and they decided to restrict traffic in the areas around schools and other public places. Parents weren't allowed to drive their kids to school by conventional cars, but only by EVs (Electric Vehicles) and bikes.

After this great victory for healthier air in London, Nicholas's parents came to an important decision. They had to return back to Oban where the air was much cleaner and Nicholas could focus on his studies and away from distractions. Money wasn't important to the family and that showed how united they were.

Nicholas was not sad that time and he knew that his parents loved him very much. London was for him a big adventure and a reminder that although normal people can't see air pollution we must be careful and learn from past events how to be sustainable today. Respect the environment and build healthier societies.

The End!

FUN ACTIVITIES

Colour the Hero and draw a sustainable transport for him to use on his everyday commute to school. (electric car, bike, public transport, walking, etc)

Colour the Hero and draw a sustainable energy source for him to charge his electronic devices. (Solar panels, wind generators, etc)

Colour the Hero and draw where he has to throw his litter.
In a recycle bin or in a conventional bin

Share with the help of your parents one of the previous drawings that you coloured and drew on a social media platform like twitter or facebook by using the phrase #NicholasEyesight.
You can use the QR code below to speed up the process.

DICTIONARY

A

Accompany (verb) go somewhere with someone
Annoying (adjective) causing irritation, bothersome
Anomaly (noun) something that differs from what is standard

B

Busy (adjective) having a lot of things to do, unavailable

C

Constantly (adverb) continuously over a period of time, regularly
Conventional (adjective) traditional, common
Correlation (noun) connection between two or more things, association

D

Discreetly (adverb) in a careful manner

E

Ecosystem (noun) a community of interacting organisms
Emit (verb) produce gas/radiation, release, exhale, pour out
Epiphany (noun) a moment of sudden realization, idea, flash
Essential (adjective) crucial, important, necessary
EVs (noun) electric vehicles
Eyesight (noun) a person's ability to see, vision, power of seeing

I

Instrument (noun) device, equipment, gadget

K

Keen (adjective) affectionate, interested in, fond of

M

Measurement (noun) calculation, evaluation, gauging

O

Ophthalmologist (noun) a doctor who treats disorders and diseases of the eye
Opportunity (noun) circumstances that makes it possible to do something, chance

P

Particles (noun) tiny portion of matter like dust, tiny piece
Particulate Matter (noun) extremely small particles, aerosols
Profitable (adjective) moneymaking, financially rewarding, or financial gain
Proof (noun) evidence, a fact

Q

Quality (noun) the standard of something as measured against other things of a similar kind, classification

R

Research (noun) investigation, experimentation, testing, exploration
Respiratory System (noun) is a biological system consisting of specific organs and help us breathe
Restrict (verb) limit, keep under control, regulate

S

Search Engine (noun) a site or application that help us find information on the internet/online, like Google/Yahoo/Bing
Sensation (noun) a physical feeling
Sustainable (adjective) having an ecological balance

T

Tickle (verb) pet, lightly touch

U

Unaware (adjective) having no knowledge of a fact, unknowing, unconscious, heedless, uninformed
Unconditionally (adverb) without conditions or limits
Unique (adjective) individual, special

V

Various (adjective) diverse, different
Vast (adjective) very big, great, enormous, huge

W

Weird (adjective) strange, unnatural, supernatural, unearthly, mysterious

29932902R00026

Printed in Great Britain
by Amazon